AF430122

T H E

Last Days

O F

King David

THE

Last Days

OF

King David

A NOVEL

Richard Chandler

Copyright © 2022 by Richard Chandler. All rights reserved.

Layout by Rachel Newhouse for elfinpen designs.

Cover Design by Ms. Amelia S. Greene for Penoaks Publishing

ISBN: 979-8-84728-091-4

One

KING DAVID WAS now old and stricken in years; and though covered with clothes he oft complained of feeling no heat, whereon his servants offered alternatives to warm him, but this he refused, as if the sharp chill he felt helped him to focus, and stay sharp. And sharpness was needed in this twilight time, for his son Adonijah much coveted the throne, and looked to usurp the kingdom with exalting himself with fifty chariots and a like number of horsemen before him, in all manner of rowdiness, himself saying in his inelegant way, "I will be king!", just in case his aspirations were not altogether clear.

Reports of Adonijah's lavish spending and rumors of his self-aggrandizement echoed through the halls of the palace of Jerusalem, the gossip from both his supporters and detractors, til it was a virtual certainty the king must know of them; and, he did. The stories of his eldest surviving son's fifty chariots and like-numbered horsemen soon became worse than just an embarrassment, this flouting of traditional relative frugality and the seemingly-modest presence of the ruler of Israel, the inheritor of the horned altar of the twelve tribes. Even more concerning, however, was this son's impatience for his father's exit, and the following vacancy on the throne.

Such impatience was not seen in the king's other candidate to succeed him. Solomon was the eldest surviving son of Bathsheba, and the son most-favored by her (mothers shouldn't have favorites, they say; but most do)—he was now a full-grown man, and he knew himself; he was reverent and respectful, strove to be wise; but yet spoke of it not, which his supporters saw in him, and saw the good works, too.

Now Adonijah for his part never offended the throne before, and he too was respectful of his father, the king—there was no black blot on him, no stain on his reputation to be wiped clean. At that time in the kingdom of Israel there was no tradition affording the succession of the throne to the eldest son, but that was most often the case—it was to be expected, like the next war; and as there was no earthly reason not to elect Adonijah as successor, nor neither was there a certainty to it, but that it came within the discretion of the ruler. As there was no assumption of succession for the elder son in Israel the king would name the next sovereign; therein lay the crisis.

Adonijah saw his ascension as inevitable; still, he secured the support and alliance of Joab, captain of the host, and of Abiathar the priest, and made it that they stood with him as a kind of ready-made cabinet, as it were, to strengthen his claim. I already have the army and the priesthood, Adonijah seemed to say; I'm ready from Day One.

Oh, but not all the powerful, nay—for Zadok and Benaiah stood not with him; nor Shimei, nor Rei, important voices each of them; nor did Nathan the Prophet side with Adonijah, his voice more important still, as his carried with it the eerie second-sight. And one voice above all these did not stand to support Adonijah.

Bathsheba did not support him.

And while Adonijah sacrificed and oxen and sheep and richly-fed cattle to celebrate himself, he called on his brethren the king's sons and the mighty men of court to join him—all but Nathan the Prophet, Benaiah of the sharp sword, to most conspicuous of all, his brother Solomon.

Well, Nathan took notice; so he thought himself to consult with Bathsheba on this very matter— notes sent from servant to servant would reach her, and so following a note from that servant to this came her reply, that she would see him in her reception room the following morning.

Bathsheba's reception room was the size of some kings' throne rooms, with soft couches and ample torchlight and tables with bowls of fruit and goblets of wine here and there; paintings of natural scenes decorated its walls, sweet incense perfumed the air, and soft cushions of every color rested on the wooden chairs, and this, mind you, was only her meeting-room.

Bathsheba was already waiting when the prophet arrived. She was still beautiful even in her fifties, with just a little gray in her dark hair, and laugh lines that graced her dark eyes and around her lips—her makeup was not overmuch, just a little around the eyes, and a touch or two on her high cheekbones; and the pastel linens she wore rested light on her, to cool her even in the heat.

Once they sat together Nathan spoke. "Have you not heard that Adonijah thinks he reigns, and seems to think that David our lord knows it not?"

When she raised her eyebrows in assent, he continued. "Therefore let me come, I pray ye, and give you counsel that we may save your life, and should it come to that the life of your son, Solomon."

"Why say you so?" Bathsheba looked at him quizzically, for she had never before regarded Adonijah as a threat. "David's eldest has never challenged the will of the throne til now, and has ever been respectful and forthright."

Perhaps it's impatience, or the proximity to power that poisons him."

"Possibly," she said with a sly expression.

"E'en now the elder son gathers many supporters around him, including Joab—why would he enlist the head of the army, but for to use him, and use it?" He touched her hand, a gesture most unusual for him. "You must go—get you unto King David and say, as you swore unto your handmaiden that Solomon would rule after you and occupy the throne, then wherefore should Adonijah reign?"

"Know ye that he does," she asked, "or might this be some show for some other, unseen purpose? If it not be so, might this show then be one of yours?"

Nathan stiffened, as if insulted; he knew better, for she was one who said very little lightly, and this matter was of the gravest for the kingdom. "My queen, you know I am apolitical in these matters, nor have I a personal interest in which of David's sons ascends the throne—but I fear Adonijah means to cut down any rivals to his power once it is his, and I have no such fear in regards to Solomon."

Bathsheba regarded Nathan a moment, and weighed his words. "You are a prophet, do you speak from prophesy?"

"No."

She considered his words. "I understand his courting of Abiathar, the high priest; but why Moab—*why* Moab, when we have no active enemies at present? In a peaceful transition Moab would stand neutral."

"He would be necessary were the succession challenged—invaluable, in fact."

"Any action taken internally would be an affront, and Adonijah is quick to temper," she said, more to herself than him. "Have you spoken with anyone else about your suspicions?"

"I broached the subject with Zadok; but little was said, as we were interrupted by someone neither of us knew, so we fell silent."

"Where is Zadok now?"

"I know not; at temple or his house, or possibly neither, for he told me not."

"Then you do not know his mind," she guessed.

"Go to the king," Nathan urged again, "and while you yet talk with him I will come in after you, and confirm your words."

She gave an ambiguous look. "I cannot say they come from second sight, only from suspicion," she cautioned, "and should you convey any more than you've just told me here, the king will know of it."

Nathan paused. "My queen, if I had claimed the reverse, you would have more cause to doubt—that you don't suggests your own bias, is that not so?"

She dismissed this. "The two brothers are very different; and any inclined to one party readily accepts any ills assumed to the other. I will not cleave family bonds in vain, nor will I pit one against another to the king, more especially given his frail condition. The single thought is monstrous."

"It is—but, as it is true what I have said, should not the king know of it? Do storms clouds gathering not foreshadow a storm?"

Bathsheba thought of the needless pomp Adonijah displayed of late, his infrequent visits to his father, and certain rash and careless statement made by him in her presence, or mentioned by others; but then, behavior was a far cry from opposing the king's will, or worse a lawless bid for the throne.

"I've always known you to be trustworthy, and never have you given me cause to doubt you," she said, finding her resolve. "I will relay what you've said to the king; and come with me that you may do the same, and answer any particulars David might have as to what you know, and how it's known."

"I know my fears," Nathan quietly said.

"May the Lord God grant I am wrong in my suspicions, and I've troubled you for nothing."

"Not for nothing, even if you are wrong," she said with a warm and reassuring smile.

"Come, Nathan—we will to the king without delay."

Two

AND BATHSHEBA WENT unto the king to the king's chamber, where he was; King David was very old, three-score and ten, no less, and laying in bed though it was midday. His gray hair came down curled to just over his shoulders, thick and unruly, and his gray beard gave him the patriarchal appearance of someone like Moses, only without the angry glare—Jacob, maybe, or perhaps the often-jovial Isaiah. He wore a light blue linen in bed, a color that flattered his now-pale skin tone.

He was awake when Bathsheba entered his chamber; awake but seemingly drowsy, for his gaze was lazy, and his hands on his perfumed sheets trembled slightly—not shaking like someone seriously ill, but the occasional tremor was noticeable, especially for someone as keen-eyed and familiar as Bathsheba.

And he was not alone in his private chamber, for the fair damsel Abishag was also in his chamber, she who was selected for the king's harem and conveyed to the palace for the specific purpose of being the king's companion, and moreover to rekindle the life in him by being with him. And though this rekindling didn't occur in the way the king's supporters expected, Abishag did prove a good, loyal friend, a fine companion and capable caretaker for the ailing ruler, and spent most of her palace time with him as a friend. So, in this regard she did in fact revive and rekindle the heat of life in the king.

When Bathsheba entered Abishag was seated over to one side, mixing scented oils and creams into a bowl; she stood and bowed, but Bathsheba took practically no notice of her.

Even as Bathsheba bowed and did obeisance to her lord David sat up, now more attentive. "What would you," he asked.

She said, "My lord, you once swore by god unto me, saying, 'Assuredly, Solomon your son shall reign after me, and sit upon my throne'—and now, see where Adonijah seems to reign, and my lord seems to know it not!"

He started as if to speak, but her urgency moved her first. "And he has slain many fatted cattle and sheep, he's called all of your other sons to celebrate him; and Abiathar, and Joab, captain of the host—yet Solomon, our son, he has not called. And know you, my lord, how all the eyes of Israel are on you, to tell the people your subjects who will sit on the throne after you."

Once more David moved to reply, but she continued. "Otherwise it shall come to pass that, when that times when you yourself are called to sleep beside your own fathers, that I myself, yea, and our son Solomon too, call be counted offenders to the crown. You know my lord what this might mean, even to danger of our lives."

At that moment Nathan the prophet came in, and bowed, and said, "My lord the king, have you indeed said, Adonijah shall reign after me and take the throne? For he has down this very day, and slain oxen and fat cattle and sheep..." Nathan then reiterated all that Bathsheba had spoke, though a little more calmly; then said besides, "Not Solomon, nor I, nor Zadok nor Benaiah has he called to his feast—is this thing done by my lord, who has not made it known who'll sit on his throne after him? Is this affront not meant to speak, and loudly?"

King David waited; when no more was spoken he raised his hand to request his turn.

"Bathsheba," he said, his voice unsteady and raspy and not at all like the rich tone of years past, "by the Lord who lives forever and redeems the soul from all distresses, even so I did indeed promise that Solomon our son should reign after me. I said so then, and, say so now. "I know now this news about Adonijah, which was whispered rumor but not known before," Bathsheba came closer and took his hand, and stilled its tremor. "I would my lord the king would live forever—I would pray he *could* live forever, but that will not be."

"We're not meant for forever," he replied, and gently squeezed her hand. "Isn't that best?"

"Yet, why meant for this?" Her quick glance told what she meant. "The lion weakens and passes in just a season; the leviathan i' the foam knows no decay, but sleeps and so passes away—why should Man's light dim for so a so long a time, and in such sad decline as this?"

"Let he who knows never tell me," the king said; then to Abishag, "Call to me Zadok and Benaiah, will you, and bid them both come to me...thank you."

Bathsheba watched her leave. "She bows beautifully—I wager she does everything beautifully."

David smiled. "I can't speak to everything," he replied, "and wagering can be prove costly."

She smiled. "I'll bet you never wager."

David gave a noncommittal shrug. "I have so much to lose, Sheba."

Nathan stepped back a bit, a little embarrassed by the familiar exchange. "Should I wait without, my lord?"

"No, no—I would speak with you, too; I count you among my trusted friends, and more, I always feel better when you are by. Friends are a medicine for a sick man."

"I'm sorry you're not yourself, my lord."

"Don't be, *someone* had to be me."

When Zadok and Benaiah arrived, both dressed in the gold-fringed robes of their high offices, Zadok spoke first. "What is your will, my lord?"

"I want you to officiate at the election of my son Solomon at Gihon; let it be without delay," David said.

"But my lord, we cannot."

"Why not?"

"Solomon is not nearby, nor is he here."

"Well, how 'not here' is he?"

"He is at Gibeah," said Benaiah, who sounded somewhat embarrassed; he was a thick-built man, quite tall, and had the nervous habit of munching and nibbling finger foods when not directly in conversation. "He is looking into some tax discrepancy involving the disposition of grain."

"Is that not the role of the exchequer?"

"Solomon is with the exchequer, my lord."

"I see; well, recall him then; take some of my servants, and bring him down to Gihon to anoint him." David then rose from his bed. "I would proclaim him to the succession without delay; so go at once, gather him up, and so travel to Gihon with haste."

"My lord, you cannot name him to the succession without the high priesthood present," said Zadok, a thin-faced, white-haired man who knew more about Jewish law than most of her judges.

"No; so go get Solomon, and bring him here—once we name him you proceed on to Gihon."

He sighed, as neither priest moved at all. "Is 'without delay' unclear to you?"

Zadok glanced at Benaiah, who was munching some nuts; he then pointed out, "High Priest Abiathar must also be present—and he is currently entertained by your eldest son Adonijah."

"Then the entertainment must be cut short," said Bathsheba. "What business has the high priest of the temple with the eldest prince, excepting a celebration counter to tradition?"

"It is certainly no official function," Zadok told them.

"I will secure Abiathar," the king said. "You will gather up Solomon, and together you'll go, yes? And one other point—I want Solomon to ride upon a mule to Gihon."

"A mule, my lord?"

David nodded. "Adonijah rides in a gilt chariot and is announced by a troop of horsemen—I would not have Solomon travel so. I don't ask that Solomon ride the mule the entire way, but let him enter the city in a show of humility."

"That will make an immediate impression," Bathsheba said, with an approving smile.

"It will take more time," Benaiah mentioned, "and also will give him time to think."

"Who—Solomon, or Adonijah?"

"Time may well serve them both," David said, the rested again on his bed. "Go now, and tarry not; and thanks to you both."

As the priests left the chamber they motioned Nathan to join them, which he did.

"There are rumors that Adonijah means to move on the throne," Zadok quietly said. "He has much support in-and-outside the palace, but I hear he no longer trusts in the king's judgment. The king is so full of age, and is unwell, and his judgment might be seen as clouded—this could afford Adonijah his opportunity."

"He will surely know of the king's decision ere we depart for Gihon," added Benaiah.

"Do you believe he will act?"

"I know not, Nathan; but you know him best— would he impede his own brother?"

"I think he will not move til he's ready," Nathan said, "and that time may very well be now. I'm told he already assumes the ruling authority in Jerusalem, and beyond, even as far north as Endor."

"Then you doubt not, but suppose he won't accept Solomon's investiture?"

"He has the support of Joab, as well as Abiathar; and Joab heads the army—it's not Adonijah's dissent that concerns me the more, but his."

Three

BATHSHEBA STEPPED UP to the palace roof via the North zigzag stairway, and briefly walked its pavilion, through the amber-banded green pillars and under its multicolored awning. Was this her fight, she wondered, as she looked to the sun half-hidden in the clouds—she was a foreigner, would always be, even if her life ended in this land; and her son was a capable man, she and David had made sure of that—still, if he as the future ruler were under threat so was the kingdom, and she knew well how conflict spread like a conflagration, and how hostilities both made and broke alliances;

this she knew very well, as well as did the ailing king.

She came down after several minutes, wound her way through half-shadowed corridors and short walkways to the King's Royal Quarters, hidden inside intricate pathways like a pharaoh's resting-place in some pyramid—the posted guard just outside it knew her of course, and stepped aside for her.

Bathsheba sat on David's bed as he snuggled again under his cover; such a familiar move seemed to discomfort Abishag, who was cutting linen strips on the other side of the wide chamber. Bathsheba noticed the look on her, and smiled. "Should I be more properly distant," she asked, and without irony.

"Are you asking me?" Abishag was quite surprised. "You are Bathsheba!"

"That gives me no right to embarrass you," she replied, and stood again. "You care so well and so faithfully for the king, Abishag—you are family."

"Now you do embarrass me," she said.

"I meant to." She turned to David. "There's much I would say to you, and some privately—perhaps you could ask her to, I don't know, fetch more oils or something."

He hadn't spoken yet when Abishag did.

"I find I need a special ointment for this new lotion," she claimed. "May I depart?"

David smiled. "Of course—thank you, Abishag." Once she had gone he said, "She has the hearing of an elephant."

"And that's I assume the only trait they share," Bathsheba said. "She is very beautiful, David—and, so young."

"She's older than she looks."

"Thank God," Bathsheba said. "But I've noticed as I get older that 'young' fits for the older and older, have you noticed?"

"It's worse when *everyone* is younger; I can't imagine having been Methuselah." He reached for her hand. "What would you discuss with me?"

She sat on the bed again. "So…just how old is she?"

"I don't actually know," he huffed. "She seems old enough to know herself."

"Then she's older than me," Bathsheba said.

David glanced the way where Abishag had gone, then met turned again to Bathsheba. "She's not what's on your mind, lily—what is?"

She smiled to hear his pet name for her; it brought back many memories. "You don't believe you'll rally from this latest illness, do you—is that why you're so suddenly concerned with the succession? Is it Adonijah's indiscretions, that stain your family name? Is it both?"

"Why is he doing it," David asked, but wasn't asking her.

"He clearly means to provoke you."

He sighed, in part coughed. "Clearly he thinks my time is nigh; that's why he's moving to consolidate his power—and he knows he would be second put up against Solomon, both in achievements and in my subjects' regard. He would plan to stop him up, somehow; I would, if I were him."

"Do you think he sees our son as a threat? They were never at such odds before."

David thought a moment. "Everything changed after Absolom's death—factions appeared, loyalties turned, and the future of Israel no longer so easily seen; it touches all my sons, but I think Solomon more than the others. It changed him, I think, and changed our relationship, his and mine."

She studied him. "Does he hold you to blame?"

"Does he? You know him better than I."

"No, surely…" Bathsheba brushed her long ringed fingers across his. "He does see us differently, David; he loves his brothers, too. He understands about Absolom."

"And, you, do you still blame me?"

"For Absolom?"

"For Uriah."

Her warmth withdrew then, suddenly, like a rapid ebb-tide. Uriah was her husband when David saw her beauty and simply took her; soon after he arranged for Uriah to be betrayed on the battlefield, his own troops deserting him in the center of the conflict, and so Uriah was left alone to be slaughtered by the enemy, and thus the way was cleared for David to possess Bathsheba. "Is that what this is about, that you think I come to hold you to account?"

He set his milky eyes on her. "I have always feared it these many years."

"You choose to ask this now? *Why?* Are you seeking absolution, so close to the gate?"

"I know that you know," he managed.

"You don't know what I know," Bathsheba snapped, "nor how long I've struggled with this; and only now you confront me, when you are so ill that only a monster could view you harshly?"

"We have spoken of this before," David returned. "This is not about forgiveness; it's too late for that."

"What, then?"

"If you fear insurrection, as the kingdom faced with Absolom, then so do I; but his cause was solely driven by a desire for power—do you believe this is something else?"

"Is that so important now," she argued. "We cannot let dissent take hold. Israel has enemies on all sides, and we must not allow civil strife to weaken her further, when her opponents sniff for weaknesses at her gates. This is the vulnerability Adonijah would exploit, this fear that internal dissent might wind up in an external collapse."

David sighed. "What then would you suggest?"

"A joint rule," Bathsheba said. "One son as king, one as regent—such arrangements have succeeded in kingdoms larger than ours, including Egypt; you would split the kingdom peacefully, force your sons to work together; and where there differences could not be bridged some consensus could be found among the royal advisers; they would kept at an uneven number to avoid any impasse.'

Sensible, perhaps; but the king found it unlikely to succeed. "Adonijah would never agree; if for no other reason than those advisers chosen would inevitably reveal biases —and if my eldest did agree, who would rule over Jerusalem?

You cannot divide the holy city in two…my lily, do you believe Solomon would accept such an arrangement?"

"He might, if it came from me; I can talk him into anything."

"Hardly fair—when you cough, you sound sweeter than the Spring rain." He smiled. "Were I to offer this solution to Adonijah, you then do the same with our son; were one to agree, it might go far in persuading the other."

She considered this. "Adonijah will be the harder; he even now assumes a regal power not yet bestowed—you'll be asking him to give up what he thinks is already his."

"But yet is not," David said, coughing a bit himself. "He can't very well miss what he doesn't yet have."

"That's a nicety he may not appreciate—why give up half once you claim it all?"

"He doesn't rule over all, that's the point; and it may come, that he rules over half, or nothing."

He paused. "Would Solomon take his people into war?"

Bathsheba kept her dark eyes on him. "I am not Israeli, but this place is my home—I would not have my people fight, and die for no better cause than power. And such internal division leaves the kingdom exposed to her enemies without, and surely both your sons see that."

"Adonijah will listen to reason," David asserted. "He inherits nothing who ruins his own prize."

"Empires are built on ruins," she countered.

"Well, my aphorism *sounded* good," David groused.

"Do you think Adonijah will agree to this?"

"At his age I wouldn't have," he answered, in a sad voice that seemed to be fading away.

Four

TWO SERVANTS ACCOMPANIED Benaiah to the royal storage house where supplies of food and linen and some weapons were kept, and the trio were brought to where Solomon was—he was atop a ladder propped against a wall, just under the second-story floor, moving jars set in rows.

"Prince Solomon, it is Benaiah," announced the palace lead sentinel. "What are you doing?"

Solomon glanced down, still fiddling with a half-empty jar. "This is too lightly-filled," he replied. "There have been reports of tax anomalies, and what is found—many of these grain sacks are half-full, when they are listed as filled…this is carelessness, or fraud; it must not be allowed to continue."

"If you don't climb off that ladder, you may not be allowed to continue," Benaiah said, munching on some seeds. "Why not let some house staff do that?"

"And, if they are behind it," he reasoned, "and if they misrepresent the value of common grain, what else might they misrepresent?"

"Could it be that those small sacks are too inconsequential to bother with?"

"I'd not thought of that." Solomon climbed down, and wiped dust from his hands. He was a comely man in his early thirties, his black hair in tight rings around his handsome face; his eyes were hazel, like his father, and his laugh lines were pronounced for that age. "I am not this suspicious by nature, but the exchequer reported discrepancies in tax revenue; I thought someone should check."

Benaiah nearly laughed. *"You?"*

"You were busy," he replied. "So, if you've come to help, —"

"I've come to fetch you," he said. "The king your father wishes you to return to the palace at once, at the request of both your parents—this tax matter will be addressed by someone else, I know not who, but someone."

He tensed. "Does this involve Adonijah?"

"It does."

"I will return with you at once."

They drove two chariots back, the servants in Benaiah's, and he and the prince in Solomon's silver-gilded chariot; they drove past long-lined the olive trees and apple trees, quince and strawberry groves of early Spring, to the wide and flower-lined royal road that led to the palace. "The matter is a delicate one," Benaiah said loudly, as they bumped along.

"Will my brother Adonijah be there?"

"I sincerely hope not," he replied.

When they arrived through the high ornate turquoise gates to the palace grounds, they were met by high priest Zadok, who carried scrolls in hand. "Your brother is expected soon," he told the prince, "as sent for by the king; and he will come, if only for curiosity."

"Benaiah looked concerned. "Is it grown so bad, that you think he'd refuse his father?"

"No; no, I wouldn't think it," Zadok told him, but something in his voice failed to convince.

Solomon knelt in the interior by the palace doors, as was custom; he and Zadok then proceeded to the queen's royal chambers, where his mother awaited him. Solomon bowed in obeisance, and stood before her table where she offered him wine. "I come at your request, mother."

"Sit; please." Bathsheba drew a long breath, and smiled kindly. "Did my request interrupt something important?"

"Nothing that will not wait. What is the matter, that draws a summons to the palace for both Adonijah and myself?"

"We are all aware that your elder brother has begun assuming regal powers, that he parades with a goodly host throughout the capital, proclaiming himself king," she said with an air of disdain. "That he should not, needs not be said; and more, that he has begun assembling a coalition of powerful ministers, including Joab, to support his claim—and all this, without my sanction or acceptance. Is this known to you?"

"I knew not of the extent of his presumption, no; but yet, he must realize you know about his actions. What explanation has he given?" Solomon waited. "None?"

She glanced away, keeping her voice steady. "We can only assume he means to take the throne illegally—unless, we suggest a co-regency over Israel."

"A joint kingship?" he fell silent a moment.

"Would such an offer not be bowing to pressure, and set a template for future insurrection?"

"Is not the alternative inviting civil strife," the queen countered. "Adonijah still assembles his faction; he has powerful support. Perhaps he uses David's late illnesses to his advantage, and if so, it may be too late to rein him in without moving against him."

Solomon leaned closer. "Are you posing only the two alternatives?"

"I see no third way," Bathsheba said. "Would you accept acting as co-regent if David and I should support it?"

He took but a second to respond. "No; it cannot be. Israel must be unified under one voice, and inspired by a single vision—once there was dissent or division arisen inside our walls, the Hittites or the Ammonites will know of it, certainly the Egyptians, and take advantage. No; whether Adonijah should lead, or I myself, the ruler must front a unified Israel."

"What if your brother accepts?"

"Then I would consider it, but only if I rule in Jerusalem…have you spoken to him?"

"We will, this day; emissaries are already dispatched to bring him here." She said 'emissaries', as though Adonijah were already a governing ruler. "Know you, too, that chariots and horse are being prepared to take you to Gihon for the holy anointing—you shall rule in Israel, my son, whether alone or no."

"I will need the proper garments, and—"

Bathsheba smiled. "They are already collected; so get you ready, as you and Zadok leave within the hour."

He started to turn, then stopped. "Might it be helpful if I speak to Adonijah? We have always been on best of terms."

She thought not, and said so. "To what avail, my son? His late behavior is so beyond the scope, and he poses as though his father was already dead, and his election certain; no, he will openly oppose you, or worse only appear to agree…yet, why this sudden approbation of power to him comes hitherto unseen in him." She paced a few steps, then faced Solomon again. "Do you think it was in him all along, and this willfulness rose up at provocation, like some deep sea creature on the hunt?"

"I never saw it in him," he answered. "If there all along, it was well hid."

"Perhaps it is in all of us," she said. "Now, go; get you ready—you must to Gihon, and time is short."

Hours later Adonijah arrived to the palace, and there met with his father and Queen Bathsheba in the grand reception hall— and yet, despite the sumptuous food laid by, the finest drink shared all around, and even quince and dates and honey cakes on trays as inducement, the notion of a co-regency didn't fare any better there. "Absolutely not," Adonijah said in an excited voice. "It cannot be, must not be; Israel must be ruled with a firm hand, and that hand must be unhindered. Is it not so, that other nations agreed to co-rule only when weakened by factious divisions, or religious strife? Is God's own nation to be seen as one of those? No!"

Bathsheba smiled slightly. "You're opposed, then?"

"It would be calamitous," Adonijah asserted.

He was a square-built man, shorter than Solomon and with much red in his hair and beard, and a harsh light often in his eyes. "And, who would rule Jerusalem? Two men cannot own the same jewel, unless it is cleaved."

"It was just a thought," David muttered.

"I know that you disapprove of my late actions, father; just as I know, you've sent a convoy to Gihon to anoint my brother in preparation of investiture."

"How do you know that?"

Instead of answering directly, Adonijah chose a pomegranate from a bowl, and took a bite. "The army and the priesthood stand with me," he claimed, "and many ambassadors, who grow uneasy with your rash decisions these several years—they know your time is not long, and move to stave off the disaster that's sure to come, if the inexperienced and indecisive Solomon takes the throne."

"He is deliberative, not indecisive," Bathsheba defended. "And if you see the king as too quick in judgment, and your brother too slow, how is your bent towards reckless abandon any better?"

"What you call abandon, I call resolve."

"It was the word 'reckless' you should have qualified," she told him. "You must listen more closely, if you would rule."

"I will have ambassadors to listen for me; and while I may not be the poet you are, my lord, I have not the weaknesses of a poet."

"You're not missing anything," David said.

"That's *not* the point I tried to make," Bathsheba whispered to him.

"Power is how to defend the nation, not persuasion; not for its own sake, but to quell dissent before it ferments," Adonijah stated, and finished his fruit. "You rule by insistence within, and intimidation without—this is how Israel must go into the future."

"You expect us to intimidate Egypt?"

"She poses no threat at present," he dismissed, "Rameses will do nothing while the Hittites nibble at the banks of the Red Sea."

"And, after?"

"We stray from the main," King David said with an impatient gesture. "I fail to see why you dismiss co-rule out-of-hand, when you and Solomon have ever been close."

"He is a good brother; that does not make him a good king. And the simple fact that I garner so much support is so short a time surely attests to my fitness to rule."

"That's sophistry," Bathsheba said. "That you assemble many to fish with you, doesn't make you a good fisherman."

"And being born the son of a fisherman surely doesn't," he replied.

David sighed, already tired. "We had thought to prepare an embassage for you, to take you tomorrow to Gihon—should it stand down?"

"I plan to prepare my own, father; I thank you, but I would not be duplicitous in this, and seem to go along, when I do not. My way is best for this blessed country, and by God's grace you will see this to be true."

He did not directly reply to this, but rang for a servant. "We will dine soon; you will sit by us, I trust, that we may discuss this further."

Adonijah declined. "I am promised elsewhere, please pardon me; when next I come, perhaps..." Then, "When is my brother expected to return?"

"The day after tomorrow."

"I will come then, that we may all speak together concerning the future of the kingdom; til then, I would take my leave."

"Until then," David echoed; as his son departed the servant entered, and was dismissed with a wave of the hand. "When Adonijah returns," he said, "he will come with terms and conditions."

"He was impertinent—if one can be impertinent at his age...he is willful, something I didn't see in him before."

"He is infected by the juice of kingship—he sees the prize is in reach, and he will not abide the time between; that, lily, is not a good trait in a king."

She looked at him. "What will you do?"

"What will Solomon do," he asked her.

Five

ADONIJAH'S PRIOR APPOINTMENT was with Haggam, the ambassador to Assyria, and with Aleazar, ambassador to Edom, in search of support from them; this was the reason he did not dine with his own family, his attempt to secure greater political support and financial aid. And he gave them sundry weighty reasons for them to back his play—weighty, if not altogether honest.

"You both know my younger brother has never led a legion," Adonijah told the elder statesmen. "He has never mapped out a strategy for battle, nor headed a troop of men against superior odds—this must surely put into question his suitability to lead the great Israelites in this trying time."

Haggam nodded at first; then asked, "Have you ever led such a troop?"

"That is not the issue," Adonijah said. "His youth and lack of life experience must count against him; so, too, his inept attempts at diplomacy, which required on two occasions the intervention of his father."

"I heard he was called on by the king to lend aid to certain negotiations," said Aleazar.

"And, those negotiations broke down," Adonijah hastily added, "no thanks to Solomon—he clearly lacks the eloquent persuasiveness his father once had."

"His father is yours, too."

"But not his mother," he replied. "Bathsheba is not an Israelite, and so has shared many of her strange ways and foreign customs to Solomon—he is not like David, any more than David is like our great King Saul."

"Is that altogether bad," Haggam wondered.

"Saul made many outright blunders, and the wars he waged for obscure and questionable reasons cost our nation many young sons."

"You are missing the point," Adonijah told him. "If we allow Solomon to rule, who is himself ruled by a foreigner,—"

At that moment Abiathar the priest entered the meeting-room, and motioned Adonijah aside. "My lord, Prince Solomon will soon arrive at Gihon, there to be anointed in high ceremony, for which I am requested—he then will return to Jerusalem with the election."

"This is most sudden; so, King David *does* move to undermine me."

The gray-haired priest spoke quietly, with some caution. "You could proceed to Gibon yourself; once there, I myself could anoint you at the southern temple. This puts you and your brother on equal footing before the people."

"Not so, I lack the voice of the king—without his approbation my claim lacks foundation. My father is old, he is no longer who he was—but he is still king, and without his blessing my reign will be seen as illegitimate, where Solomon will come ushered in with hosannas."

"When then is your remedy?"

He wasn't so sure. "I cannot openly challenge his authority, not when he has our father's voice to lift him—but, what if Solomon cannot reign?"

"How would that be?"

Adonijah turned to the ambassadors, who were talking then to each other. "My good friends, there is a matter of state to which I must attend, without delay; so, let us adjourn this meeting for the evening, and reconvene tomorrow over the midday meal—is that acceptable to you?"

"It is, my lord," both said, and so they departed.

"Where is Joab? I would speak with him."

The priest directed him to Joab, who was conversing with a silversmith about the firing of inlaid designs. "Joab, a word, look you."

"Yes, my lord?"

He then drew Joab away to a more private place. "Tomorrow Solomon is anointed, and travels back to Jerusalem; if something were to happen, in the time twixt now, and then, there might not be a Solomon to return to Jerusalem."

"My lord!"

"He is not king til he's proclaimed," he continued, "and that proclamation comes from the palace; if Solomon never reaches the palace…"

There was a terrible silence; terrible, for both men. "He is your brother, my lord."

"I know the curse that befalls that man who kills his king," Adonijah said, "and I would not have my younger brother become king; and neither, I think, would you."

"He is anointed," Joab mentioned. "Were he to be struck down before he returns to Jerusalem, the question's resolved.""

"Were he struck down—if not killed by some accident, nor some random event, but by a sword—I of course would not rest til someone was blamed; after all, he is my younger brother."

"Suspicion must fall on you."

"And on my supporters; so, let us fervently pray that Solomon is not so obviously killed, and not die by someone's sword," Adonijah said.

"Perhaps some natural occurrence might alter the dynamic, even to convincing others that the intervention be God's will—and who's to say nay, when all that occurs must occur by God's will?"

"Then you suggest that Man's will is but God's; what boots it then to worship, if by your logic it's God glorifying Himself?"

"What grocer thinks it so far, what sailor or nurse would follow such a line of reasoning?"

He paused, as if he wondered the same. "Most subjects never see the king in all their lives—what care they, if they pay out their yearly tax of an Adonijah, or a Solomon? It matters to us, general—not to them."

In Gihon Zadok the priest took a horn of oil from the tabernacle, and anointed Solomon therewith; and so the trumpets blew, and those who stood all around shouted, "Long live King Solomon!" For so he was there; but, not yet in Jerusalem.

And so the people came up after him, some playing on pipes, some twanging on cymbals or striking on drums; and this went on and on, well into the night, til there was just no sleeping nearby. And the people rejoiced, as much for having *any* reason to rejoice, and danced and spun and called Solomon's name, though truly some didn't know one single thing about him.

The following morning Solomon's procession to Jerusalem hurried into readiness, that he should arrive back to the palace before sunset; so horses were well-fed and washed-down, chariots prepared, and sentinels tested their swords for sharpness. All was in readiness by the mid-morning, and the smallish procession left Gihon well before midday.

Abiathar, who had also officiated departed for Jerusalem well ahead of the procession.

Along the route to Jerusalem the convoy came to a pinched way that threaded in-between tall rock faces, known unimaginatively as 'the narrow path'—there was a spookiness about this stretch, due not only to its high stone walls, but also for the occasional echoes of the calls of wild beasts who were up on the cliffs but could not be seen.

Only this time the eerie sound wasn't an animal, but the rumbling crack of falling stones.

"Forward—hurry!" Cried the lead sentinel, and the convoy dashed forward through the narrow band, as rocks and stones began to rain down from the upper edges and lips of the left wall. The horsemen in front and formerly behind galloped through the pass and to safety, but the chariots were slower.

They sped forward amid falling rocks, stones and shards, to where the clearing could just be seen up ahead—but then there was a snapping sound on Solomon's chariot; the suddenly shifted violently, and the chariot crashed onto the narrowed, pebbly ground, the prince and his driver falling onto the earth.

"Up, quickly!" Solomon cried. He pulled his driver to his feet, and they ran toward the clearing, rocks and sharp debris falling all around them, the dust so thick the way forward could barely be seen, but for their horses who ran ahead.

The horses reached the clearing first—then Solomon and his driver, who he helped; behind them several weighty stones still fell through the pass, roaring like hungry lions.

"My prince! Are you all right?" asked the lead sentinel.

"I am—are you well, Micah," he asked his driver.

"I will be," Micha said; he was bleeding on his left side, but not badly.

"What happened, did you drive into something?"

"No; one of the wheels gave way."

"On your chariot? All four chariots are new-fashioned, how could that happen?"

Is anyone else hurt," asked Solomon; and luckily no-one else was.

Zadok joined them, and stood beside Solomon. "Do you think it intentional?"

Solomon looked back to the clouded path.

"If it was, the evidence is smashed and buried beneath all those stones; it could never be proved."

"I could send someone to the cliff top to look for sandal marks, or any signs people were up there."

"Any traces will be erased, long before we could reach the top," the sentinel dismissed. "We'll proceed more cautiously, but we are now not far from the capital."

"You are unharmed, Solomon," Zadok said.

"Is it a miracle, that you came through this peril with only a torn robe?"

"Oh, but it's my favorite robe," he claimed.

And so that day swift-running messengers hurried back to the capital, far ahead of Solomon's procession, his mule granted upkeep at one of the finest of Gihon's stalls; and the messengers announced the impending arrival of Solomon's procession. Now, there was much noise and rejoicing in Jerusalem, too— dancing, cymbal-twanging, and all, enough to put one off his midday meal.

And so it was with Adonijah, whose guests the ambassadors could scarcely be heard above all the tumult. "Why is all this noise," cried Joab, who sat with Abiathan's son Jonathan nearby, "that all the city seems to be in an uproar?"

"It seems to bode good news," said Jonathan. "I hear, King David will proclaim his son king!"

"The *other* son," Joab moaned, and looked over to Adonijah. "It appears that Solomon has entered the capital safely, safe from harm—intact, as it were..."

"So—let us rejoice," Adonijah said, and almost with a sincere tone; but his eyes gave him away, for they betrayed far more anxiety than joy, and far more fear.

Six

SO SOLOMON WAS welcomed in the king's palace that afternoon by several servants, then Benaiah, who walked with him to the king's chambers. "First, see to it that Micah is attended to by the palace physicians," Solomon ordered, and it was done.

"It's almost a miracle you escaped unharmed," said Benaiah, who nibbled on some grapes as he spoke.

"Not entirely—with my chariot gone I had to ride in with Zadok, who talked my ear off."

"The landslide, your chariot wheel…do you think it treachery?"

"It could never be proved; so therefore, say nothing of this to the king, at least for now — as this may have been an accident, there's no need to worry him."

"If there's a threat, he should know of it."

Solomon almost laughed. "When is there not a threat?"

In the king's chamber David greeted his son warmly, with much food and drink prepared, and music playing; Solomon thanked him, and gave a gift of calligraphy-bordered parchments from Gihon, that was famous for making this, and David returned his thanks. "You come here dusty and torn," the king said, a glance at Solomon's clothes. "We are family, but you still present before the king — we are not so nomadic a people as once we were."

"I should have changed before coming in, but came only to announce my arrival. I will bathe and redress presently."

"I don't mind," David said, flicking off dust from his son's robe, "but I mean to publish you as ruler at once — you are King Solomon now."

"A king who wears some of his native soil," he replied. "Besides at a distance no-one will see it."

"I'll be next to you," his father said. "I will see it."

And so, bathed, perfumed and redressed, Solomon stood with the king at the royal balcony overlooking the great courtyard, where David proclaimed him forthwith king of all Israel.

Everyone was there—well, many were there; and nearly everyone of importance among the hierarchy, including of course Zadok and Benaiah, and most of the important figures of Israel. Queen Bathsheba was there, but not on the balcony; and David's caregiver Abishag was there, unseen, way in the back of the audience room.

And Adonijah was there, perhaps not so overjoyed as was most of the crowd.

As festivities and celebrations gathered steam and momentum, Adonijah, Moab and Abiathar met together in a sitting-room just down the hall from Adonijah's old room, when he was a youngster—there they drank wine, dismissed any waiting servant, and sulked. "We all know vindictive your father can be," said Abiathar, in an uneasy tone. "How vindictive is your brother?"

"He is ever even-handed and reasonable, that's what made him such a good target; but, I've never seen him react to a plot against his life."

"Not only him," Moab added. "There were 22 men in that convoy; and, I understand his chariot driver was injured in the pass."

Adonijah looked at him. "How injured?"

"I know not; but if he had died, I think we heard about that."

Abiathar took a quick drink. "Does he suspect?"

"I assume you mean Solomon…I've not spoken to him since he returned from Gihon."

The prince sighed. "Have you, Joab?"

"It seems, none of us have—what do you make of that?"

All three were silent for a moment. "We mustn't do this," Adonijah said. "We mustn't see danger where none exists, nor overlay our own tendencies onto others. Think it through—if Solomon told the king he was suspicious of us, you, Moab, would be in a locked room."

"And, you two?"

"We would be questioned," Abiathar said.

"As I am high priest the temple stands with me; and as for Prince Adonijah, well…but then, for you it would be an attempted fratricide, attempted murder, and possibly treason—and since your position makes you the bigger threat the punishment will fall harder and faster on you."

"I hate this conversation," the prince said.

Moab finished his wine. "So, we do nothing, and wait for the knock on the door?"

"*If* they knock on the door…"

Adonijah sighed. "We must not run—it would be like a confession; we must keep our heads, feign ignorance…'a landslide? How unlucky,' we should say; or, 'It be God's beneficence towards you, great king, to have spared you from such a horrendous and unforeseen natural occurrence…'

The gladder we are that he lived, the better."

"Solomon's no fool," Moab barked. "He's sure to see through us."

"Then, we stand between him and the king," he suggested. "My father has killed his offspring before. My brother has no proof, nothing but suspicions to take before the high court—and, the High Court will not allow him to condemn any of us without proof, of which there can be none; should he act reflexively his reign will be very short indeed. I know him, he'll never risk it."

"Then he can do nothing without a confession."

"And I am seldom loquacious," said the prince.

In Solomon's quarters, the newly-proclaimed king was examining his new wardrobe, precious silk gowns, bright-colored cloaks and trays of dazzling multicolored rings, when David entered unannounced. Solomon was still in the long silver gown he wore for the coronation, that was too big for him and draped like a collapsed tent around him. "It seems we have a co-regency, after all," he said to his father. "Are you not still king?"

"I am a proxy king," David said, in a reedy, thin voice. "I am the figurehead that fronts the ship, you are the captain now."

"And, should we disagree or divide on some important question of state?"

"I will see that we don't," David told him.

"All diplomacy should run so smoothly."

David then rested in a chair nearby. "When were you going to tell me about the landslide?"

He looked surprised. "You know?"

"Micah told Shikkel, the palace physician, who told me…Solomon, you must keep in mind that you are no longer an individual—as king, you carry a collective identity, and when you're at risk so is the state."

"All kings lead their troops into war."

"War is another matter…do you believe the incident at the pass was an accident?" Solomon said nothing. "Then you must pursue who you suspect is responsible—not in vengeance, but as an obligation of the crown."

"You argue against vengeance," Solomon questioned, knowing his father's history.

"Certainly—I've seen what it can do."

He turned to his father. "What if those I suspect are close to my family?"

David sighed. "How you proceed is your decision; but, you must act. If you do not, they very well might—indeed, must, to protect themselves, or fulfill their agenda…you can be magnanimous in rule, but you must rule."

"And if all I have are suspicions?"

"Then you wait until you have more than suspicions; but, look you—you must not wait for certainty, as that proof could come on a sword's point."

Seven

ADONIJAH WAS LEAVING his rooms that same afternoon, when he saw a small procession of palace guards pass by through the hallway ahead; and amid these guards, he thought he saw Moab, the head of the army. He hurried to the hall that paralleled his, and stepped in front of the procession. "What is going on," he insisted, "that our military leader is under guard?"

"My prince, General Moab is being taken to be questioned concerning the incident that befell the king, while en route from Gihon," said the senior guard.

"I was asking him," Adonijah snipped.

"I would say the same," Moab told him.

"Why, what has some accident to do with you," the prince asked, somewhat animated. "Is our new king out to interrogate anyone who showed him less support? This is not to be accepted—my father will hear of this; yea, and the high priest Abiathar, too."

"My prince, High Priest Abiathar is also detained, and to be questioned by the high court," the guard said.

"I see…Is anyone else to be questioned?"

"Not that I know."

He turned to Moab. "Well, you have no worry—you yourself have done nothing amiss; and, if some misguided supporters of yours might have acted rash and over-zealous, and all without your knowledge, their wrongdoing reflects not on you.

And you, you told me yourself that you spent that same time with Jonathan, brother to the high priest, did you not?"

"I did indeed tell you that," Moab said.

"Then surely the high court will not detain you long—sure, it must be they plucked your name at random, to seem as though they act in the new king's name. Let this not trouble you, Moab."

"We should proceed, my prince," said the guard. "The general is awaited at the hearing-room."

"Of course…worry not, general; I will speak with my father about you."

And, he would, or not right away—first, Adonijah left the palace and hurried through several short and turning streets to the temple, and once inside hastened to the altar of Yahweh.

This was a square column of stone with a hornlike protuberance that rose from each corner; in the sight and witness of several attendant priests and acolytes Adonijah caught hold of the altar's horns—this action invoked the ancient tradition, by which a man under suspicion could claim the protection of God against any pursuers.

This move was quickly reported to King Solomon. "It is verified by witnesses, my lord, that your brother has laid hold of the horns of the altar," said one of the temple priests. "And more, that he said, 'Let Solomon swear unto me that he will not slay his servant with the sword'."

The king sighed. "Has he?"

"You could still hang him," Bathsheba kidded; she was there with Solomon in the throne room, which was lavishly adorned with mosaics of natural scenes on its walls, and many thin furs of different colors laid across its floor. The priest Zadok was also present, sipping a goblet of water.

"Why would he claim the ancient rite if he was innocent of wrongdoing?"

"That question is immaterial at present," Zadok told him. "He has claimed the protection of Yahweh, and that is inviolable."

"He may not be killed at the altar; that doesn't mean he cannot be arrested," Bathsheba clarified. "And if he violates the sanctuary laws in any way, such as himself killing any who come to detain and remove him, the protection of the altar is forfeit."

"Might he yet be innocent," Solomon supposed, "and fears that appearances might go against him, that he might be condemned wrongly?"

"If he means to alleviate suspicion, this is a most curious move," she said.

"Both Moab and High Priest Abiathar are held on suspicion—either, or both could implicate your brother in hopes of easing their punishments; and, your brother's opposition to your election is well-known. I might fear it, were I Adonijah."

He turned to the beautiful Bathsheba. "Mother, what would you do?"

"I would hold my hand until I knew more," she said.

"But at the least, you must detain your brother," Zadok said, "or he is surely for Damascus or Median, where you cannot reach him. Bathsheba is right, that the altar horns protect his life, but not his freedom."

"I like it not," the king said. "My first act on the throne would be to arrest my own brother; and why?—Because he objected to my father's decision to over-leap his eldest son for the throne. It surely gives my opposition more cause to hate me."

"And if he goes not to Damascus, but to the Hittites—or south, across the Sinai into Egypt?

What if his next move is not only against you, but against Israel?"

"Could he do something so perfidious?"

"We would find out too late," said Bathsheba. "Would it not be best, to keep him from finding that out himself?"

Solomon agreed. "Detain him—then let it out that we act not to punish, but prevent; and in so doing, set no stain on those in our inquiry til the truth be known. Let any who act with guilty intent fear our sword, even to the sacred altar."

"The temple priests may object to even this as sacrilege, my lord."

"Then let them object; they have been curiously silent about the Abiathar's detention."

"It's possible some are glad on it," Bathsheba suggested.

Zadok disagreed. "They see he acted afternoon political interests, not in service to the temple—this is not Thebes, where the priesthood openly serves the will of the ruling factions."

"Adonijah may have thought he acted for the best," said Solomon. "He has so far as I know, led a blameless life til now."

Bathsheba gave a sideways glance. "If he ordered an assault on your convoy, that's hard to see in an innocent light."

As she spoke, as if on cue, the palace physician Sikkel entered the throne room. "My lord, you requested to hear news of Micha, your chariot driver…"

"Yes; approach, please." Solomon waived off Sikkel from any formal gesture. "Tell me, how fares he?"

"He is much worse," Sikkel reported. "Much sand and grit had entered the laceration in his side, and threads from his shirt—his wound is infected, and he now suffers with a high fever. It's possible, he may not live from his injury."

The king grew concerned. "Can you minister to him, and rally him?"

"My physicians try, good my lord; but, this fever coming on so soon concerns me."

He understood. "Do all you can for him, Sikkel—he is a good man, and has a young wife and child. Thank you."

As Sikkel departed Zadok said, "If young Micha dies, and the landslide was caused by men, then they commit murder."

"And, that would Micha sustained might well have been your wound," Bathsheba reminded him.

"Should Micha die, you will no longer be free to simply forgive this, it would be the highest injustice to his family—and those who might yet move against you will say, you excused this killing because your brother was involved."

"I know," Solomon said, his fingers to his lips, and his eyes fixed on the throne room door through which Zadok departed.

"Your God will work through you," Bathsheba said after a moment. "By Him, you will see what course to take."

"*My* God?" He looked at her.

"You are now king of Israel," she said.

His will is now reflected in your own—it is through you, now, that He reveals Himself to His people."

"But nothing has changed," Solomon said.

She lay her hand over his. "The king is more than collecting the tax, or deciding policy; you now speak for God's actions, even as the temple priests speak to His will...in the eyes of your subjects, Solomon, you act as He would act—so, you had better act well."

Eight

THE FOLLOWING SPRING morning was as light and lovely as any one could imagine. The soft early sunlight shone in clear golds, a cool breeze wafting through the crisp air, sparkles on the petals of flowers and amber rays slanting through the high branches of green trees, a morning that spoke of renewal and rebirth over the rich lands in and around Israel.

David walked out to the palace and surrounding grounds in the early morning, white puffy clouds in thick clusters overhead and the sun peek-a-boo behind, still low in the curving sky, a birdsong and river-morning that stays with you months later, when you need it.

The main courtyard featured a statuette-surrounded fountain at its center, and tiled walkways that led to gardens either side of the palace proper; at every corner of the high outer wall stood folded awnings which were extended over much of the courtyard in summer months.

A vague fresco over the courtyard ground depicted scenes from the Joseph story, from the dark enclosing pit, to the triumphal reunion of the vindicated Joseph and his brothers.

But for distant birdsong it was a quiet morning—palace guards kept a discreet distance, talked amongst themselves, or played at dice; the spearheads that topped the high outer wall were more decorative than useful as a defense, and they gleamed and glittered when the ascending sun reached the right angles. From a certain spot at a certain time of day, these spear-tips sparkled light stars along the high wall top.

So many years, David mused as he wandered toward the western garden—so many years he's lived inside these high walls and within the vast and labyrinthine palace; so many crises faced down by Saul, and so many he faced himself, never knowing if his choices and decisions were sound, were right...you try, weigh your options (those open to you), and you guess.

You put the great nation first, that sometimes means putting her at risk; you trust what you believe is true, sometimes more than that which you know is true—unwise, but sometimes necessary. You choose a course of action, and you go—sometimes seemingly right off a cliff, and often not knowing how deep is the river below.

Sometimes, not knowing if there's a river down there, at all.

The gardens were in bloom that morning, midway in the first week of April, and profuse with lilies, primroses, laughing daffodils and shy crocuses, golds and reds and bursts of purple amid green leaves and flowering thorn, all in quiver on the soft breeze. The varied scents lent the air a rich perfume, lush on the breeze and sweet as the mist off the breaking waves on the shore. The play of colors and shades and varied shapes, all dazzling and dizzying in a small sweep of life, many flowers and plants whose names David didn't know, and never would—like strangers in crowds of familiars; welcome, even inset in the curling rush of shades, and some perhaps unnamed, at least in Hebrew.

And, so brief—their blooms so brief, their stays so short in this curious cycle, the wave we all ride along the inclusive, encompassing tide of life, before the braking wave crashes roaring on that stranger shore before us all.

So many years…those early Springs; and all that nonsense about Goliath, and the lucky shot that changed David's life forever—Goliath's, certainly. Oh, he was tall, over seven feet, is true; but not over three cubits, which was nearly 10 feet, no. Had he been, David could never have made the shot he did, not from that angle.

Nor did the Philistines fold and flee at the fall of their tall, over-dressed leader, but fell back only for a short time—it was later negotiations and certain key concessions that ended the conflict.

The myth of Goliath came in handy later on, and so David felt content to let it play, especially when it lent advantage to the illusion of Israel's military might, aided by angels, inspired by God, that little Israel not be overrun under the heavy chariot wheels of the Hittites, or caught up on the spears of the great eternal Egypt, when even her ageless pharaoh lived on through generations, seemingly the living body of his empire's ceaseless longevity.

And the myth was useful, too, inside the nation's borders. Saul knew the truth, but knew besides, that David did go alone to face the giant and, unaided by little more than stone and spirit— did he send David up there to that battle line in the same way David would later send Uriah? Did it matter anymore?

Now, his son Adonijah was under arrest— Haddith's son, who spoke sharp words unto David's harem, and so won a quick displacement. Another son had moved to seize the throne, and possibly plotted against the life of his brother…mercilessness, the familiar knot in the family line, the darkest common thread that linked Boaz to Nashon, Aron to Perez, dating back through to brothers of Judah. It was even in Abraham's willingness to sacrifice Isaac on the rough hewn altar, all over a voice he thought he heard.

And, what was it in Man that made him so susceptible to the call to slaughter, to the heartlessness in it, the barefaced evil of it? Why was it that Man is as ready to torch a garden and scorch the ground, as he is to plant the seeds, and nurture the tendrils? Is it mere expediency, or ignorance, or willfulness? Is it Man's pride that pushes them to the irrevocable, so is something missing in his nature that should be there, isn't, and who takes the blame for that?

Does Adonijah know that being king is not so good a calling as he might think?

Bells sounded; bells stood on posts placed before the entrance way to the palace gates, to signal an arrival to be ushered in—in this instance, additional medicines and medical supplies for Shikkel, who was tending Micha; two riders on horseback then entered the complex, and David knew one to be Rinossa, another physician who'd worked with Shikkel in the past. It bode not well, that they came in haste so early in the morning.

David entered the palace by small and innocuous side doors, and wound his way to the offices of Benaiah, who headed security for the complex. Benaiah stood and bowed, but David scarcely took notice. "Good morning, my lord—you look as though you didn't sleep well."

"I don't sleep much these nights, which may be just a quality of age."

"I sleep far more than I had, and I am one year shy of you."

"A telling year, evidently," David said. "Have you spoken with Moab, and with Abiathar?"

"I have, they deny any involvement; however, I also spoke with one of Moab's long-time aides—he told me Moab dispatched a dozen soldiers to somewhere outside the city yesterday morning, and no written orders were given."

David was intrigued. "Benaiah, we both of us know 'the narrow path'—it would require about a dozen men to create rock-slides all along its thinnest stretch, would it not?"

"It would, my lord."

He sighed, hoping he was wrong. "What is the hour?"

"It lacks of eight."

"Where is Adonijah now?"

"He is returned from the temple, and is under guard in his old quarters."

"Tell him I will talk to him in two hours, after breakfast—I would not catch him off-guard."

"Only, it costs you the element of surprise," Benaiah said, and offered the old king a cup of water.

"He knows we'll question him, it can't be too much of a surprise."

"Oh, but the wait brings anxiety, and the anxious often—uh, am I arguing against my own point?"

"When we're next in chariot, I'm driving," David said and took the cup. "The least we might do is give Adonijah time to prepare—I would wish it, were I in his place."

"He will lie," Benaiah cautioned. "Moab and Abiathar did, I'm certain of it."

"He might lie to the king—but that, I am not," he replied, "and I know not yet if he would lie to his father."

"Would he not," the counter came, "when is own life was at the stake? Is he has done what we suspect, filial loyalty is not his first concern; if he'd lie to the Court and to the king; and especially if he truly believes he's in the right, despite the laws…"

"Your point is inconvenient; and however much I want to deny it, I cannot. And yet, Benaiah, I can't believe him to be so duplicitous."

"Or is it, you can't believe he'd dare try to deceive you?"

"I know him, Benaiah—if he does lie to me, I'll know it."

Nine

ONE GOOD THING about the palace of Jerusalem was the food—even the cleaner-ups and the newbie guards were afforded the best of foods; this was something of a jest in the capital, in fact, that the stout guards of the palace were so well-fed they must subdue intruders quickly, as they could never run them down. It wasn't much of an exaggeration, either; but unless the evil-intended came from the Arabian desert, they wouldn't want to run much either under the bright Jerusalem sun.

And as prince, even while under guard, Adonijah enjoyed a splendid breakfast most Israelites would envy; after, he read a scroll recounting the Exodus, and the long perilous journey out of Egypt—he read calmly, as if he had no worries, while he waited for his father to come visit him.

When David did come, he set the scroll aside. "All blessings on you, Father," he said with a deep bow. "I was reading just now of Moses leading our people into Canaan…do you remember telling your sons this story, and how you'd act out certain parts, and change your voice to suit?" Adonijah smiled. "In your version, Moses sounded like a bull cow!"

"Not everyone who can sing, can act," David said, by way of apology. "As a boy you had a fear of drowning, and I couldn't understand it, as that is one story where Israelites need have no fear of drowning."

"Was that why you read that one story?"

"Oh, there's far more to the story than the crossing the sea," David said, "and truth be told, I can't remember why I recounted it when I did."

"You told us many times all about Moses— 'There's kinship there', you used to say…yet even as an adult I saw it not, the remove from then to now being so great."

"Not so great, and our family isn't in a direct line…I find it sad how God spoke directly to us then, and does not now.'

Some think Moses carved the tables himself," the son said, "that he assumed the authority that went unquestioned."

"Burned into the stones—twice?" The father looked skeptical. "How did he manage that?"

"Forty years in a desert…how did they manage that?"

David sat near his son. "Adonijah, I came to ask you about the landslide at the pass—the chariot driver Micha was badly injured there, and is like to die; if he does die, anyone involved, however tangentially, must be condemned."

Adonijah looked him squarely in the face.

"No-one can condemn me for what I did not do, and I never ordered an assault on my brother's convoy."

"That is sophistry," his father remarked.

"The powerful but let their wishes known, then wait for those who curry favor to act on their own.

You wanted Solomon stopped, and but for God's grace that incident would have stopped him."

"Can I help it if I'm lucky," he replied.

"What instructions were given to the dozen men Moab sent out of the city early yesterday?"

"How should I know?"

"Was Moab acting on your behalf?"

"Do you believe I would sanction an assault on my younger brother?"

"Did you?"

Adonijah shook his head, not in denial, though, but in disbelief. "This family kills its own, doesn't, Father? And I don't only mean Absolom; you didn't raise us in togetherness or familial warmth, but in duty to nation—and, why? Was I overlooked, because my mother fell out of favor with you? Haddish was strong-willed, self-reliant, qualities you found attractive at first; but when she defied you she stained not only herself, but me. And, is the careful and savvy Bathsheba so superior, when she accepted so readily the murder of her husband, and that after her infidelity—how was that good for the nation?"

"Solomon is innocent of that," David said.

"And, so am I," Adonijah countered, "innocent of my mother's defiance of you."

"Your mother and I grew apart."

"You bedded three other women the year you were with Haddish, there was no closeness to grow apart."

"Never presume you know someone else's struggles, especially in something as personal as love."

"You never loved my mother," he accused.

"You used her as you had so many others— 'David of the 100 women', I would hear at the court; and I knew, my mother was only another one of them."

David had to pause, in part to align his thoughts, and curb his anger. "If your fight is with me, it is with *me*—not with the nation; and when you act on the life of the elected king, you stand against the entire nation."

"He is wrong for Israel," Adonijah warned.

"He is young, and idealistic, and he will lead our country into a war when she is not ready."

"And so, you acted to stop him."

"I did nothing," his son said, "and you can never prove to the High Court that I did what I did not. The Law follows intentions, not benefits; it judges plans, and not dreams, and a man cannot help what he favors."

His father sighed. "We will learn which soldiers were sent to the 'narrow pass', and of those twelve one of them will reveal the truth—when that happens, that testimony will serve as proof for the High Court."

"That soldier could be lying, and you have no means to determine whether he is."

"We will speak further on this."

"Will we?"

David picked up the scroll, and momentarily glanced at the writing. "May I borrow this? Is it well done?"

"Well, the writer is no Asaph..." He smiled.

"It is well enough, though I think in this telling the Egyptians might well prevail."

Oddly, David smiled in return. "That would not surprise me...Adonijah, I will myself speak to the High Court for leniency, but know you, I am no longer king."

"Say what you will, Father—my conscience is as the flowing water."

Near midday Solomon and Bathsheba left the palace and rode chariot into the busy, bustling center of Jerusalem, which buzzed and pushed all round its many thousands of people; the horses that pulled the chariot wore the distinctive white and purple plumes that denoted royal ownership, so that all but the youngest knew not to molest them or their charges in any way.

Both Bathsheba and Solomon wore light, flowing linens, nothing ostentatious nor gaudy, and this by design, or else they might face much molestation, if not outright begging; this was more for her benefit, for he looked much like everyone else, but she in both beauty and bearing suggested if not demanded a kind of regality—she *looked* rich, come down to it, and would if she wore a sack cloth.

The merchants of the central marketplace could smell it right off, as she and her son visited the open air bazaars and open-air markets that flourished near temples and schools, and especially in those wide squares surrounded by selling booths and kiosks.

In fact on one occasion, the very same head scarf priced at ten shekels for a lady in front of Bathsheba was priced at thirty shekels for her.

"Might you be mistaken," Bathsheba asked the young bearded merchant. "Thirty shekels seems high to me."

"No, no, I assure ye," said the merchant.

"I in fact discount this for you, for you are so beautiful!"

"We may just discount him altogether," Solomon remarked.

"Twenty-five, and you have the prettiest golden scarf for your silky black tresses," the merchant urged.

"Let us say fifteen, and I'll not report you to the Merchants' Collective for gouging."

"Fifteen, then—and, it's a steal."

"It certainly is," she agreed, and gave a sidelong glance.

As she moved on, and Bathsheba gave the scarf to Solomon, he laughed. "He of course has no idea who we are," he said. "It is odd, isn't it?"

"It's liberating, though I might not feel so safe were you not with me." They took in the many wares and now and then got jostled by shoppers or passers-by. "Let us buy some wine, and perhaps something sweet."

They soon found a seller who sold both, an old merchant who'd had few customers that day—it was perhaps because of his sign, that depicted a camel in a desert. "You are most welcome, most welcome," he said with a flourish.

"How may I help you this fine day?"

"Two bowls of wine; and, something sweet," Solomon requested.

"Fresh apples in honey?"

"Perfect!" Bathsheba cooed.

He brought these to them, suggested a spot nearby that was shaded by awnings, and also gave them cloth strips to protect their linens while eating. "May your meal be blessed." he said.

Solomon thanked him. "What do we owe you?"

"Nothing—your mother, so I think, is the loveliest woman I have seen this day, and it is a pleasure simply to meet her; surely, she is as lovely as the queen."

"Thank you," said Bathsheba with a big grin. "Thank you!"

A time later David visited Benaiah once more in his office. "I've spoken with Adonijah, he says his conscience is like flowing water—I assume he doesn't mean silty and muddied."

"He knows equivocation," Benaiah replied, eating little pieces of apple. "Where do you suppose he learned that?"

"I could never imagine," David lied. "But, his anger—his anger runs deeper than I ever knew, and that makes him dangerous...my own son. Is the High Court in readiness, do you know?"

"They convene tomorrow, as they purpose."

The old king looked lost. "I told him I would speak for him, Benaiah—I all-but-promised I would argue for leniency, but in his eyes I saw only hatred and resentment—and, it's earned; I strove to build that hatred, block by block."

"That's past," Benaiah reminded. "His is the guilt now."

"No; no, I cannot shrift it so; if you abuse a lion, and the lion strikes you, the fault isn't his.

I know Solomon will be the better leader, I *know* it, I think Adonijah knows it, too; so then, why do I feel this poison course through me?"

"What works on you is your age, which is great; and your burden, that bends you. King Saul saw what his ruthlessness as a tool when he smote in the name of God—he seldom asked, I think, if that's what God wanted."

"How can we not ask it," David posed. "We stumble through brambles in the dark."

"What was done, was done for Israel, it does no good to doubt that now."

"Or, is now the only time?" David asked.

Ten

DAVID KEPT MOSTLY to himself throughout that day, questioning what was best to do, whether he should speak with Solomon, and intervene—and should such intervention fail, what would that mean? Adonijah's involvement was yet unproved, moreover, denied by the eldest prince of the realm; and no, David didn't believe him. And what if the aide who reported Moab's 'dozen troops'

lied, and for some yet-obscure unknown reason wanted to set up Moab, and to those predisposed to believe the worst of him?

Is evil intent guilt in itself—if so, all men must bend to the harsh judgment, and few so guilty, perhaps, as David himself; the worst of old age, they say, is now you know who you are.

So David retired to his royal chambers with its silks and many colored cushions and its plush furniture, and suffered. There was something in him now that bubbled and burned, it ran along the lines and veins of his limbs, it curled round his bones, and squeezed; it didn't feel like sickness, sickness was something better borne.

After all these years, and even now when his fingers were no longer as nimble as they once were, David still kept his harp in the quarters.

It was not the same harp, mind, as when he was young, nor the one he played decades back, when he was his most prolific in psalmistry; this was a new-ish harp, a few years old. He tried to teach Solomon to play it, this didn't go well; then he tried to teach Abishag, who is apparently tone deaf— quite something, when you think about it, since playing a ten-string harp is not so hard.

In any event, David brought down the harp from its niche in the wall, strummed a few times, and started a new psalm:

> *'My Lord, why do I know so little of you,*
> *And after so many long years?*
> *You spake to Moses, who carried the tablets*
> *That gave your laws unto Israel;*
> *And to Noah, who braved the risky waters,*
> *And Jonah, who was in leviathan,*
> *And so delivered of the sea—But speak not to*
> *   me who loved and served you,*

And did oblation to you every day.

'Why are you grown so distant now,
Who felt so near when I was younger?
It's now I need you most of all,
That troubles crash all around like waves,
And this vessel I man is taking water,
Is pitching and like to split.
My offenses are many; yea, too numerous
For my weakness to excuse,
But what can I do now for them, now that —'

His voice was not what it was—in truth, not what it was just a few months ago; and as if to drive the point home, Abishag stepped quickly into his quarters then, with a look of alarm. My lord, are you well—you sounded as if in distress!"

"I wasn't, but I am now." He set the harp down. "I was singing a new—I was trying to sing a new song, that came to me over these past hours…it is not yet ready, evidently."

She was so embarrassed she wanted to vanish—not just leave, but disappear like a ghost. "Good my lord, I meant no disrespect, truly; had I known that was singing—you *have* sung before, haven't you?"

The guard who was posted in the hall outside also popped in then, one hand on his sword. "My lord, is everything all right—I thought I heard whining in here."

"I was just—whining?" David blanched.

"Did it sound like a ghost," she asked.

"It, it sounded like nothing human," claimed his guard with some alarm. "May, maybe the ghost of some wild beast!"

As Abishag tried not to laugh David pursued.

"And do you believe in ghosts?"

The guard relaxed, as he saw all was secure.

"I didn't before now," he claimed.

"All's well in here, thank you."

"But keep listening," Abishag needled as the guard returned to post.

David grinned, which spoiled his mock anger—Abishag knew him so well, knew what she could say (which was just about anything), and understood him; this last endeared her as much as her stunning beauty. "Perhaps not," he said, a glint in his eye. "Perhaps, now that I'm no longer ruler I'll start hearing more honest opinions."

"I'd worry not," she said, coming on over.

"People should encourage fledgling artists."

He raised his eyebrows. "Would you like to hear the rest of the song?"

"Let's not go *too* far," she needled, and quick touched his hand. "Your song is sad, why?"

"My bell, do you fear the future?" This 'my bell' was his pet name for her, for a flower's bell.

"Everyone fears the future—do you fear your God?"

He nodded. "I fear His judgment, and I know it is nigh."

"So it is with everyone," she said. "Time is only time—a day, a year, ten years…in all, there's only one moment that matters."

"The moment that you die, my bell?"

"The moment that you love, my lord."

He gave her a look. "Had I known you Shunammites were so beautiful *and* so wise, I would have conquered you decades ago."

Now she gave a look. "Then it's just as well that I'm exceptional, isn't it?"

David wrote out the last lines of his new psalm then, before they were forgotten:

'But what might I do now, as I am old
And the chill in me fringes all I touch with
*   frost?*
Recompense for loss never changes what's lost,
But yet there's always joy in that that's found.'

He showed it to her, and she gestured that it would serve—no better than that, but would serve. "My bell, we've known each other over a year now, and I still don't know how old you are—very young, yes, but how young?"

"I don't mind my pet name," Abishag said, her eyes smiling, "but I am no-one's pet."

"You do pet me," he pointed out.

"You have me there." She tried and failed at keeping a serious look. "I am nineteen, my lord, very nearly twenty."

"Do you know how old I am?"

"I know how old the world is...God thought the world into being, when He became lonely; then Man appeared, to comfort the world. It's what my people say, and they say that every people see their own creation story in creation itself."

David held her hand, to show her thanks; as his companion she already had everything she wanted provided for her. "Perhaps it's best that we had no intercourse, that you are not infected with me."

"Do you want me to say, 'Oh, what could you mean', or, 'Oh, you cannot mean that', so that you feel better?" She set those lovely eyes on him. "Your Queen Bathsheba says, 'the greatest gift is ever the truth', and she is my guide and my North star—so I say, oh my lord, you cannot mean that."

He hugged her, coughing even as he did.

"You are my good friend," David said. "I have so many best friends, I hardly have room for more—but I'd like to squeeze you in."

Abishag smiled. "I'll make myself small."

"Much smaller, and you might not be," he exaggerated, for while Abishag was shorter and lighter than he, she was there, all right; and what was there, was wonderful.

"I could write out the words to your new song, if you would like," she offered, lightly stroking his skin. "I promise to transcribe word for word, and improve nothing."

David shrugged. "I will comply *only* if you promise to improve what you would," he said.

Eleven

The high court of Jerusalem convened the following day, when the sun was midpoint in the sky—one earlier case involving the alleged theft of grain sacks from the Capital Granary was heard first; then, the three-judge panel of legal scholars were presented the case against Moab, head of the army, and Prince Adonijah, son of David.

And the Court said unto Solomon, who stood as accuser, wherefore say you that the first man of Israel's army planned usurpation, and doing evil to the king's anointed? And wherefore say you, that your own brother and kinsman plotted to have you killed? These are heinous charges indeed, most serious accusations you bring to this Court—if you have proofs to present that indict these good men, then bring them forth.

Elsewise, said the Court, the king's bonds must loose, and these men be free; yea, and seek recompense for the unjust words of the Crown.

Then did the aged David step forth, and this unsteadily—but his words were strong, and rang through the tiny courtroom like tolling bells.

"We submit in writing the reasons for these our accusations," said he, "and more, we make no stinging statements lightly, but lit by the truth from inside—for you know, each of you, when I set you up on this high bench where now you preside, I believed in the forthrightness and clear-sightedness of each of you. We come not to condemn, but to correct; and if this rift might be mended without the spilling of blood, let it be done; and if accommodation might be made between these my sons, that like strife be not rekindled, let that be done, also."

What accommodation, asked the Court—Obia, specifically, who was senior.

"I would speak," said Adonijah, "as prince of the kingdom and the rashly accused—should this Court look not to condemn us, let Moab be placed again at the army's head; and more, as I am prince and look not for Solomon's throne, then grant me King David's companion to wife once he's gone, and no longer needs her."

"This is outrageous!" Cried David, who turned quickly on his eldest son as if to strike him.

"Abishag is not some mule, to be passed between owners!"

"Some say she is," mumbled Moab.

The court then asked whether Abishag had been consulted on this matter. "She will be," said Adonijah, "shortly after this Court adjourns."

"We will consider the request," said Obia, and motioned the tribunal. "It seems only reasonable recompense."

"It is not," said Solomon. "Abishag is not only a paid companion, but friend to the king; yea, and to Queen Bathsheba, too. If you rule irresponsibly in this I will dissolve this court, and vacate your ruling—and more, I will order the dealing with Moab and Prince Adonijah as *I* see fit."

"You would make Israel a lawless land?"

"I would rid her of an unjust court," he said.

"As to my perfidious brother I say, should he show himself a worthy man, I will spare every hair on his head—but if wickedness is found in him, he shall die."

"We will consider all that's said," Obia pronounced, and adjourned the Court.

Solomon turned to his brother. "Go you home," he hissed. And, he did.

As David and Solomon set to return to the palace, the old king paused by the horses. "His request is meant to get at me, Solomon, to undermine me; but, I would not have Abishag become a pawn," he said.

"A what?"

"A pawn—it's a piece from a board game that's played in Persia; it's much like the game of senet played in Thebes and Abydos."

"Adonijah knows his history, that the taking of a king's companion is seen abroad as a direct challenge to his rule; and here, too, in several quarters of the kingdom."

"Abishag might not understand it, she being of Shunam—she may not realize the implications in my brother's request. Should I speak to her about this?"

"No, let Bathsheba speak to her of this—and should she raise no objections to the match, then please respect her wishes; Adonijah was ever a good man, a good son—I don't see him evil in him, even now. So let the decision be hers, and support that decision once it's made."

When David struggled to mount his horse Solomon asked, "Are you well enough to ride?"

"God grant, as I'm not strong enough to walk," he replied, in a fading voice. "Inform me of the court's verdict in this once it's published. The decision is yours to follow or disobey, but you must be resolute, and never waver; and in this, you know my mind."

"If I defy the High Court in this, I'll need many weighty reasons to justify the defiance to the people."

David rubbed his tired eyes. "You could say it was the will of the old king—perhaps his last."

Not long later Bathsheba met with Abishag in the Queen's lavish apartments, and there explained the matter where it stood; and they shared fresh fruits, and good wine, and Abishag listened as the queen expressed both sides of the question before her and, more to the point, how Abishag's life would suddenly change, whether or not she agreed to the marriage after David's death.

It wasn't so much like sisters, this talk, more teacher and pupil; and Bathsheba who believed in honesty above all, was brutally truthful with the young, beautiful companion of the aged king.

"The conflict between David's sons is for the throne," she told her, "I have never known Adonijah to be cruel, or heartless, not in my dealings with him—but if he is willing to murder, I would never trust him; and know, therefore, even I cannot protect you every night of every day."

"What reason is there to trust him once I'm wived to him," Abishag asked. "His promise to me will do nothing to stop his bid for kingship."

Bathsheba thought a moment. "If we should work to fracture his coalition, he will have no good support for his bid; but this cannot be done quickly."

"Our marriage would buy you time."

"I cannot ask that of you," Bathsheba said with a kind smile, "nor is this your fight—your personal loyalty to my, to David extends only to him; if you choose, you return to Shunem upon his death with many treasures, richly deserved."

"But that will not help you," she replied.

"Has there ever been anything between yourself and Adonijah?

"No; nothing—we have met, of course, and spoke courtesies between us, but nothing more."

"But has he betrayed any interest in you?"

She couldn't quite say no, but, "Most men notice me, my lady, they have since I grew tall and more womanly; but I cannot help that."

"It is your lot in life," Bathsheba kidded.

"You may make light, but I only hope for so understanding a husband when I wed."

"Speaking of…?"

"If David agrees, and if you agree, I will stay to serve the precious Israel that he loves so well. I will support you however I may."

"My David has a good companion in you," said the queen. "You make me proud."

"Nay; no more, or you make me cry," said Abishag. "Let me know how best to help you."

Twelve

THE NEXT MORNING David woke flushed and feverish, the tremors in his hands worse than before, his vision blurred—so concerned was he that he sent for Shikkel. He drank several cups of water while waiting for the palace physician, but his throat was still dry; his vision improved, but the shaking in his hands remained.

Shikkel had been asleep, and it took him some time to prepare, though the servant who fetched him told him that, while David's condition had worsened, and how, he seemed to be in no immediate danger (the servant's own father showed similar symptoms, and lived with them for over a year).

David was much recovered by the time Shikkel arrived, but was understandably unnerved. Shikkel came with a sack in which he kept liquids, salves and sundry other medical items, and sat on his patient's bed. "Have you been sleeping?"

"Not well," David said, "though that may as much from conscience, as sickness—I did have a nightmare, which might explain my headache."

"It must have to be quite the nightmare—what did it entail?"

"I dreamed I came unto Heaven, but God knew not who I was—He didn't recognize me at all; no-one did, not Saul, not even Absolom, who seemed to not understand my words when I spoke out."

He checked his pulse. "So, loquacious even at the Gate, are you?"

"I wouldn't let something so little as death quiet me," David said.

"So, how did the dream end?"

"I was admitted at the last only because God knew I must belong there, or I never would have met Him…I was then led by an ethereal blue flame to a smallish house, which I took to be in a kind of suburb."

Abishag entered then, and came straight to his side. "I heard you were unwell, how may I help?"

He smiled. "Stay close to me, you are ever the better tonic."

"I like that," Shikkel mumbled in faux jealousy, and took out a string of bright-colored beads.

"Now, follow these beads with just your eyes...good."

Then Solomon came into the chamber, followed by Zadok the priest, and security overseer Benaiah. "Are you unwell, Father," the king asked. "Your servant looked concerned."

"I am feeling better."

"The High Court has ruled that they will not rule," Solomon reported. "Senior Judge Obia cites lack of evidence for presenting a case, which returns the matter to the purview of the Crown."

"But the status of the Crown is the matter."

"Perhaps they fail to see that," Abishag said.

"No," David said, "They see it very clearly."

"Father, are you well enough to scan this letter lately come from the Ammonites?"

He sighed. "This is your purview now, Solomon."

"It is addressed to you by name, from the prince—it may be personal."

"I have nothing personal to do with the prince of the Ammonites," Davis groused, but took the letter. "It—it is a state matter, proposing an increase in cloth and flaxen trade...ah, he asks after you by name, Solomon; so, answer him yourself."

"Is there something you need," Zadok asked; and when David glanced over to Abishag added, "something that anyone *else* might provide you?"

"I'll not have all this crowding around," Shikkel chided, and the men moved back a bit.

"This is a sick man."

Abishag could still crowd in, of course, and did. "Would you like more water?"

"There is one other matter to address," said Benaiah, "concerning Moab."

David touched his companion, nodded about the water, then turned to Benaiah. "What is this matter concerning Moab?"

"He says he fears for his safety under palace arrest, now that Solomon reigns—he asks he be confined in Gibeah."

"I wouldn't mind being confined in Gibeah," Abishag said. "It is lovely there in Springtime."

"It would decentralize the opposition leaders," Benaiah mentioned. "This may be sound strategy on his part."

"He seems to concede that his faction cannot prevail," Zadok added.

"It is not my decision," David said with a rasp in his voice. "I would allow it, but you should properly confer with Solomon."

Shikkel mixed a liquid for his patient. "If there is nothing else, our patient needs his rest…Drink this slowly, my lord; it will cool you and help you gain your strength."

"What's in it?"

"Do you mean, everything?"

"Never mind…" He sipped as instructed, and his visitors began to depart. "My son, a word—I know how busy you are with the, uh, the transfer of rule; but I would speak with you sometime today, on matters of import."

"Of course," said Solomon. "Come see me when you like, and I'll stop all other activity."

David smiled. "Thank you."

Shikkel packed up. "I'm leaving you this soothing cream, and another potion to help ease any discomfort."

"Lotions and potions," David mumbled, pleased with himself. "What clever notions!"

Shikkel and Abishag shared a 'why us' look. "Rest today, my lord—it is most important; you'll be no use to anyone if you're obstinate."

"More than usual," added Abishag.

"I am in your hands," David said to Shikkel, though a quick glance at her suggested another meaning entirely.

Solomon waited for Shikkel in the outer passageway, and asked him aside. "How is Micha faring," Solomon asked. "One of my servants told me that you no longer worry for him."

He looked curious. "Who said I don't?'

"Zebah, who brings the bedding to be washed each day."

"Micha's fever has broken, tis true, but I still minister to him. I believe he is out of danger for his life."

The king smiled. "May I speak with him?"

"Is it an urgent question?—Then hold off for a few days, and let him rest; I don't doubt that in a week or two he'll once more pilot a chariot."

"Is his family informed?" The physician said they were. "And when he's strong enough, might he return any less surly?"

"I am not the court magician," Shikkel said.

By midday Abishag had started napping, as she sometimes did on sweet, lazy Spring days; she was beside David, the bed so wide that they were not touching. But David couldn't sleep, his thoughts crowded close around him, pushing in to be heard, vying for ascendance, memories unresolved, hopes unfulfilled, all crying for attention. So insistent were they in mind, he almost fretted that they might wake Abishag, who moved her fingers now and then as she slept.

Again, the family crisis tore at him with claws like hawk's talons, like the long curling fingers of apparitions in children's tales; these, though, dripped with the blood of David's kinsmen, and his children, and the children of Israel.

He crept out of bed carefully, as his companion continued napping, took his harp from its niche, and retired to another room; there he gathered pen and parchment, and thought to rid himself of the soundless voices surrounding him.

'My enemies are inside the gates, My Lord;
They walk the halls I walk, drink what I drink,
And eat of the dishes prepared for me.
They share the shade of these same awnings
That shelter me, and they whisper furtively;
I see their shadows blend with mine

As I walk beside the tiled garden walls,
I see them in the water, when I look into it.

'Who am I turn to when my own wrongs rise
    up
Like the shimmers of heat off the stones?
I cannot undo the past, O Lord—only You can;
And only You can undo the knotted cords
That tangle me in constant guiltiness
That robs me of sleep, and baffles me like linens
In their confounding folds.

'Am I so small that you should know me not,
O Lord? Am I another buzz in Your ear,
Like the tiny winged thing I brush aside?

'I thought I acted out of wisdom, but was it
Out of ignorance? I wanted to live in love,
But was it only wanting all this while?

'My enemies take my clothes, O Lord,
They take my cloak—My enemy wears my
    cloak and my sandals.
Lead me to understand and talk with them;
Lend me voice to plead my case, I beg You;
Let my not fall away in my iniquity,
But hear You when it's my time to speak.
    Selah.'

David looked up from his harp and parchment,
and Abishag was standing near.

"Are you hungry," she asked. "I tend to be hungry when I rise from sleeping."

"Did I wake you?"

"You weren't there," she said, and smiled.

Thirteen

AFTER THE MIDDAY meal David visited Solomon, who was in his throne room consulting with many ministers; he gestured to David that he wait, and the old king rested nearby in a chair.

"We must abide by all treaties and promises to M Median, they're promises, after all," Solomon told one adviser. "It is not just that Median is friendly to us, but her proximity to the Sinai, and more especially to Egypt, lends her more value than she would have were she, say, bordering the Black Sea—yet we agree out of friendship, and so tell her so."

"Have you writ the Ammonite prince," another asked.

"I will, and soon; perhaps tonight…what is the question with him?"

"Cloth trades, my lord."

"Yes, yes; I forgot, I won't again—do leave his letter by me, and I'll see to it. But now, my father waits impatiently for my attention; give us an hour, will you, and after I will address any further concerns."

"Including the question of geese?"

"Geese, Ullamon?"

"We have too few geese for the markets," Ullamon said in a worried tone, "even for this time of the Spring—we have found that they have sufficient gaggles in Gibeon, however; they ask that we trade for them."

"What do they need?"

"Grouse, my lord."

"Of course…well then, we'll give Gibeon our grouse for their gaggles of geese, with gratitude!" Then he grinned. "No more for now, I must visit my father; so, thank you all."

As they left they bowed to David, who stepped forward. "How glib," David said.

"I wonder whether Adonijah still wants this role…" Solomon smiled. "How are you feeling?"

"On the mend—I composed a new psalm this morning."

"Then at least, *you're* on the mend…" He shook his head. "I hope to someday emulate you in your musicianship, but as yet no; after my last harp lesson my tutor asked to join the Hittites."

"You had a tutor?"

"It is sometimes miserable to be related to you," Solomon griped. "Maybe my upbringing is to blame, maybe I should have shepherded when I was younger."

"It's not all it's purported to be," David said.

"Why did you want to speak with me?"

"I have found that very little occurs within our borders that's not known by our neighbors," David prefaced. "It is likely that the Hittites know already of the fracture between you and your brother, that could have split this nation in two; and that they might yet move to gain from this moment of weakness."

"I know that, and preparations are made even now."

My time is soon," David told him. "I go the way of all the earth; therefore be strong, and show yourself as the man I know you are. Walk always in the ways of the Lord, keep his statutes and commandments, better than I have done—His judgments, testimonies, even as writ in the laws of Moses will see you prosper in all that you do, whichever way you turn."

Solomon nodded. "It was ever my intent, Father."

"If your children take heed to the Way, walk before our line in truth with all their heart and soul, then there shall not fail to be any from out our house on the throne of Israel."

"I understand."

"One word more," David said. "You also know that there are those who acted against my throne—Joab, as one, who killed so very many; and Shimei, the treacherous. They are old now even as I am, but I would you have you not let them by, but deal with them even as your own wisdom dictates to you.

"But look you, show kindness to the sons of Barzillai of Gilead, who was kind to me—invite them to your table when you will, and extend them all graciousness."

Solomon touched him. "Your time is not so near," he said.

"I think it is; if not now, soon. I meant to speak of this before, and feel easier that I have done now."

"What of the priesthood—those inclined to support Abiathar remain in place; if they should mount a challenge in continued support of Adonijah, this situation is likely to recur."

"Then the key is to turn Abiathar, not make an example of him—leading by loyalty is always preferable to ruling by fear."

The new king seemed to concur but said, "How may that be—he chose to back Adonijah, and that won't change; if I show both men magnanimousness they might see it as weakness."

David coughed again, but gestured to put Solomon at ease. "The priesthood is governed by questions of spirit, not politics; you may have no worries there, if you show yourself to be a good man."

"A good man isn't always the right man."

"Tell Zadok to publish the attempt against you to the priests—such perfidy won't sit well with them." David waited then, not speaking, til his son piped up himself.

"Is there something else?"

"There is the question of your mother," he finally said. "She must play a key role in the court you assemble after me."

"I will be mocked, once it's known I'm taking advice from my mother."

"Not *your* mother," he assured him, "and I know no single diplomat, prince nor king who would ever dare challenge her to her face."

Solomon smiled. "I see no reason why her position at court should change," said Solomon.

"As she is your trusted adviser so will she be mine; indispensable, in fact, as she is to you."

"I appreciate that you didn't say, 'was'," David said. "I want your mother accorded all honors as befits a head of state; all, I say—as I wronged her, it falls to you to make my amends."

"If such is my charge I'll be doing little else," his son chided. "Yours has been a long reign, and there has been much wreckage in its wake."

"Yes," he simply said; what else could he say? "You have the people's affection, Solomon—I've seen it before, and often; start there, with them. If you trust in them they'll see it, and will repay that trust."

"Most Israelites will live their lives without ever seeing me," Solomon noted, "and maybe that's for the best."

"I always found it a comfort," David said.

Fourteen

DAVID HAD RULED over Israel for forty years; now, forty years is a general term in in the ancient records, signifying a vast long time—in fact, forty was a number denoting some vague lengthy while, as in the forty years the Hebrews who wandered in the desert under Moses; they didn't wander forty calendar years, and if they did, Moses had a dreadful sense of direction.

No, forty was a symbolic number—seven is another; those seven kine, seven sons, seven seas, all those. Seven meant 'some', but not as much as 'forty'—' a thousand' also didn't mean one thousand, but far more than 'forty', and the same with 'a million', which didn't mean one million…numbers then were nearly as fluid as spelling was, which was downright gushy.

But David actually did reign over Israel for forty years; seven years in Hebron, and 33 in Jerusalem, so that the years of his reign would themselves carry a symbolical value for the Jews

going forward, from the magical seven earlier, to the later 33 mirroring the lifetime of the Messiah to come, the last ruler of the House of David.

Now, his reign come to a close, and Solomon secure on the Israeli throne, David could lower the sails of his pitching skiff, and so come to rest.

He had given to his people; had taken much, too, always justifying his oft-heinous actions by claiming either divine right, which was dubious, or the justification of the State, which was worse.

He had taken terrible chances, sometimes unwisely, and sacrificed much, usually others—he learned a great deal from the reign of King Saul, and most was it not good.

But his reign established the kingdom of Israel as a major power in the region—that, by the standards of his day, was the true justification of his dicey rule. His people need not fear the Hittites much, nor the Ammonites, nor the Persians—they feared the Egyptians, but then everyone did.

And now David looked back on his years on the throne, and knew he had much to answer for.

He claimed he was always inspired when making his grand decisions, but 'Inspiration won't buy a fig', so wrote Sargon, or Ptah-hotep, or someone.

David knew, his missteps and miscues had cost his people dearly, even as his successes brought prosperity, and how the balance stands who knows save God?

That night was he sore troubled, and as he sometimes did, less so lately, he again took to his music for solace. He took down his harp, found parchment and pen, and wrote:

'Thank you, O Lord, for all you've given,
And keeping me from the snares of enemies;
Thank you for the gifts I'm given, and give,
That those I love may know they are loved.
I'm grateful for friends closer than coral,
And for the loves shining brighter than jewels,
And for a faith clearer than water.

'Thank you for my deliverance from the storms
That roar with rain, thunder, and the waves
    high,
That my poor boat's buffeted through the
    night—But I will sail though to a peaceful
    lee,
I will disembark on a quiet shore.

'Lead me, O Lord, to that far joyful place
Where worries and iniquities desert me—Lead
    me through the ruins of my past
On to a green open space of solace,
That I stand new-made in the realm of light.

Selah.'

And just as it had happened the night before, as if arranged, a beautiful woman entered his room where he had sung—this time, it was Bathsheba. She was wearing a lime-green gown over where white linens, and her only jewelry a multi-beaded bracelet on her wrist.

"Where is your companion," she asked.

"I don't know," David said, setting down his harp. "Perhaps she's flirting with one of the younger chefs for honeycakes."

"It's those full breasts, they do need feeding." Bathsheba crossed the room to the far table, where several parchment lay. "Your song just now is new?" He said it was. "If it's a confession, it lacks the confessing part."

"Those are also new," he said as she glanced through them.

"I like this one," she said and held up a parchment, but she never told him which one she meant.

"Art is good for everyone but the artist—from him it takes blood and water, both needed in his climate."

"If you say so," she dismissed, and set the parchment down. "Do you know, Zadok has been collecting your psalms and those of others; I think he means to publish them."

"I would not have those included with any others." David motioned to the parchments. "I know they're not among the best...lily, do you think that art still survives once it exists, even if only in memory?"

"I think *art* does," she qualified, and smiled. "May I keep these, for my own reasons?"

He nodded in assent. "Why are you here?"

"I came just to see you—your time is short; all of ours is, but it's shorter for some."

"Then you've come to say goodbye?"

As he spoke Abishag entered, carrying a tray with two goblets of wine, and honeycakes on napkins; she set down the tray, bowed and departed, not saying a word.

"I think she loves you, in a way," the queen commented. "She's like all the others, in a way."

David walked slow to the table, and offered Bathsheba a cake. "Are you bitter?"

She took it, and her wine. "You're soon for that place where your charm, your talent and your wealth will mean nothing…I am not bitter, nor sad." She carefully tasted her cake; not daintily, she did nothing daintily. "I'd heard it said, you are a man 'after God's own heart'—I wonder if they who said it misunderstand what that might mean."

"It makes little difference now."

"No, not so easy; you are not absolved just because you keep living." She sipped her wine.

"Do you remember the Spring we spent in Lebanon? We stayed in that little house we had of Sandia—I remember those endless open fields, the tall reddish trees, and we boated down that peaceful river…it was shortly after Uriah died."

David drank his wine and rested on the edge of his bed. "We have been through all this."

"We have." She sat beside him then. "On the day we met, when your soldiers came to collect me, took me from my home, they said I was to have a personal audience with the king; and when *you* took me I could not fight back, and certainly not draw blood—I could have been killed for it."

"However wrong it was good came of it," he replied. "Solomon came of it."

She looked at him curiously. "Do you still not see it?"

"You have done nothing wrong in your fifty years, I suppose—so for those wrongs however long ago, what can you say? I have made amends to you, again and again; and even I have not the power to raise Uriah up again."

"You misunderstand, I hardly remember him now," Bathsheba said. "David, if you know not yourself, how could you ever know me?"

"I hypothesize," he told her.

"I once swore to myself that I would never see you or talk with you or think about you ever again..." She sighed. "You wore me down."

"I have that effect on people, often after only a very short time."

Bathsheba smiled, only briefly. "Solomon will rule Israel well; he has a good heart, and that's what matters most. I will see to it that Adonijah is kept in check, should that matter resurface—but he is cunning in a way our son is not, and that frightens me."

"There's many to help you, and our son; all will be well."

"Will it? There's many who will oppose his rule, inside and outside; they stretch out their claws and will pounce."

"And Solomon will outflank 'em, or else outrun 'em—he will prevail, I know it."

Bathsheba gave him a quick, soft kiss, then turned her attention to the remaining cakes.

"Do you think Abishag would notice if none were left?"

He sighed; she was playacting, of course.

"She's a tough one, built to endure the bitterest of times—I think she could survive the loss."

As David rested on his many pillows she replaced the harp to its niche, picked up the new psalm with the others, and took only one more cake. "It's time I go; you should rest now."

A few moments after she'd gone David thought he heard the door once more, maybe she returned for something forgotten. "Bathsheba?"

He waited a few moments, but no-one came nor answered him.

That night, King David died in his sleep.

Fifteen

DAVID WAS SHORTLY thereafter buried in his city. And Solomon announced a national period of mourning for thirty days, which was largely symbolic and changed almost nothing; and Solomon's kingdom was established greatly, and a celebratory period of one week, which changed a good deal.

And during this time Adonijah, who was the son of Haggith, quickly realized that his position relative to the Crown had now changed; when his father ruled he was relatively safe, both due to distance and the ebbing of anger that so often accompanies an older age, but now Adonijah's intended victim occupied the throne, and with it the power of life and death himself—probably not good, so far as Adonijah was concerned.

So Adonijah came unto Bathsheba, and she was none-too-surprised. "Do you come peaceably," she asked, and glanced now and then to be certain that the prince brought no-one with him.

"Peaceably," he assured her, and said moreover, "I have somewhat to say to you, and you alone."

"Say on."

"You know that the kingdom was mine," he asserted, "and that all Israel set their eyes on me, as expecting the elder brother to reign: howbeit the kingdom is turned about now, and is become my brother's, who thought it his from the Lord. And now I ask but one petition of you; that being, that he grant me Abishag the Shunammite to wife. I would you ask it of Solomon, for he will not tell you no."

She stared at him. "Why—that is, apart from the obvious? She is beautiful, she is talented, but I think not overmuch; and there are fifty pretty women at court who would walk through fire to marry into the House of David."

"Why question this simple request? Is it hard to believe that I want such a lovely creature?"

It's what else you want that worries me, so Bathsheba thought; but as she faced her stepson she could not fathom it. His brother might know more; yes, in fact, Solomon might well know.

"I will speak for you to the king," she promised.

And indeed Bathsheba did go to the king, and relayed his brother's request; she told him what Adonijah said in the palace throne room, which was then free of ministers and so a private time, which Bathsheba urged. And she said beside, "He said, you would not tell me no; so intended I should say to you, let Abishag the Shunammite be given to your brother as wife."

"Why would he ask this, think you—if I cannot say no to you, and you ask for him, let him ask for the kingdom also!" Solomon stood quickly, and paced before the dais on which the throne rested. "He wants something more than her, that is certain."

"Perhaps it's what she knows about your father, or what she knows from your father. If Adonijah should mine her for information, there may be much he could use against you."

"Mother, would my father be so careless as to share with a caregiver more than he should?"

"Abishag is a very young and beautiful woman," Bathsheba said.

Solomon nodded. "He likely told her everything, then!"

"And she said herself, there is no personal history between her and Adonijah," the queen added, "So, the only likely reason for his request is..."

Solomon motioned a servant over. "Call Jenniah in to us, please."

As the servant hurried off, Bathsheba spoke in quiet tones. "This is not necessarily a bid to undercut you, my son; there may some other motive at play."

He looked at her. "Such as?"

"If your brother yearned for her in secret but could not speak, as she was companion to the king, that might explain his request."

"Even if it does, his utter disregard for Abishag's own wishes is despicable."

"But not criminal, not that."

Jenniah arrived a few minutes later; she was Mistress to the Royal Harem, and as such one of the most powerful women at court. "What would my lord?"

"Mistress, know you of any communications, rendezvous or commerce between King David's companion Abishag and my brother, Adonijah?"

She shook her head. "None at all, my lord."

"Has Adonijah ever spoken to you about her? Know you of *any* dealings between the two, aside from typical social exchanges?"

Again, she shook her red-haired head. "No, my lord."

"Thank you," Solomon said, dismissed her, then instructed another servant. "Bring Benaiah before us."

Bathsheba put fingers to lips, and thought. "Your brother may have spoken to another woman in the harem about Abishag, and Jenniah might not know—it's at least worth finding out."

"My direct, unsubtle brother? -No."

"He might see her as a link to your father, who never took her as a mistress."

"He would not know that."

"He is your *brother*, my son!"

"He is," Solomon said, but would not look at her.

A few minutes later Benaiah came to the throne room, and bowed in obeisance.

"I come as requested, my lord."

Solomon hesitated, but only momentarily.

"Know you the current disposition of my brother, Adonijah?"

"It is roundly time for the midday meal, so I suspect he's eating."

"Has he had any visitors yet this day?"

"He has—Amaziah, Chief Scribe to the Royal Office of Ambassadors; I know not the reason for the visit, but Adonijah did send for him."

"He would have a foreign communique," Bathsheba said in a quiet tone.

"I need know no more," Solomon said. "Benaiah, King David would that I defend the house he made me, and so I do—this day my brother Adonijah shall be put to death; the time and manner of it, I put unto you."

"After this evening's supper, then?" Solomon nodded; Bathsheba shivered. "It shall be done."

"It must be done," Solomon told his mother.

Then Benaiah spoke again. "My lord, General Moab and High Priest Abiathar were also hip-deep in conspiracy, and so still pose a threat."

"We will think on it," said the king.

Benaiah left, and Bathsheba stood to leave also. "Well, the killing of your own brother is not one of your *very* acts as king; it has been five days, after all…may the Lord God forgive you."

"May He forgive us all," Solomon said.

She left the throne room and walked the long brightly-tiled halls of the great palace; she left through a small side door that led to the garden. The rain had started minutes earlier, a soft mid-April rain that sparkled on the trembling flowers, the daffodils and tall marigolds, and beaded the soft grasses. Bathsheba stood in the rain for several minutes—she didn't mind the chill, nor the raindrops on her face, as they might disguise her tears.

www.ingramcontent.com/pod-product-compliance
Lightning Source LLC
Chambersburg PA
CBHW070909160726

48004CB00003B/1296